Busy Bumble Bee
Rides the Waves

Carol Hair Moore

Illustrated by Michael Harrell

To order additional copies of this book:
Order online: www.iwishyouicecreamandcake.com
Phone orders: (850) 893-1514
Series: I Wish You Ice Cream and Cake Book 2

Inquiries should be addressed to:
CyPress Publications
P.O. Box 2636
Tallahassee, Florida 32316-2636
http://cypresspublications.com
lraymond@nettally.com

Library of Congress Cataloging-in-Publication Data

Moore, Carol Hair, 1940-
  Busy Bumble Bee rides the waves / Carol Hair Moore ; illustrated by Michael Harrell.
-- 1st ed.
      p. cm. -- (I wish you ice cream and cake ; bk. 2)
   Summary: A little bumble bee rides a piece of driftwood far from his home on the Isle of St. James at St. Teresa Beach, Florida, then must ask creatures of the Gulf of Mexico to help him return. Includes facts about a variety of animals, as well as the geographic areas featured.
   ISBN 978-1-935083-06-1 (hardcover)
  [1. Lost children--Fiction. 2. Bumblebees--Fiction. 3. Marine animals--Fiction. 4. Fireflies--Fiction. 5. Mexico, Gulf of--Fiction. 6. Florida--Fiction.] I. Harrell, Michael, ill. II. Title. III. Series.

PZ7.M7824Bus 2009
[E]--dc22

                                        2009002046

ISBN: 978-1-935083-06-1
First Edition

*Dedicated to
my loving
father-in-law,
W.T. Moore, Jr.*

*He taught us all
to love St. Teresa.*

There once was a little bee named "Busy Bumble Bee."
He lived on the Isle of St. James at St. Teresa Beach, Florida.

One beautiful summer day, he was flying from flower to flower
in Nana Carol's colorful garden.

It was a cool, breezy day. He was having a wonderful time,
as the flowers were full of nectar.

He flew down by the sparkling water and landed on a piece of driftwood. Away he sailed! Suddenly he realized he was at Alligator Point. He didn't know how to get back to St. Teresa. Busy Bumble Bee began to cry.

Mr. Octopus popped out of the water. "Can I help you, Busy Bumble Bee?" Mr. Octopus exercised his eight arms as he spoke to the little bee.

"Oh, yes," said Busy Bumble Bee.
"I have come too far from home
and I need to get back to St. Teresa."

Mr. Octopus began to expel ink into the water and said, "I can't help you, but maybe Mr. Scallop can."

Mr. Scallop began to open and shut his shell with a spitting sound, saying, "I can't help you, but maybe Mr. Redfish can."

They heard a drumming sound. Mr. Redfish was singing joyfully. He told Busy Bumble Bee that he would like to help, but he could not stay on top of the water long enough to ride him home. "Mr. Loggerhead Turtle might help you!" he exclaimed.

The loggerhead turtle is a very special turtle.
There are not many left in our world, so
we must try to protect them.
We do not want to disturb their nests.

Mr. Loggerhead Turtle said, "Hop on my back, and I will give you a ride home."

They sailed across the water
as if they were waltzing to beautiful music.
The waters were calm today.

Dusk was falling on St. Teresa. The little fireflies were gathering at the dock for their nightly visit.

The fireflies, also called lightning bugs, flicker and light up beautiful St. Teresa like a fisherman's cast net filled with sparkling stars.

"Thank you for my ride home, Mr. Loggerhead Turtle," said Busy Bumble Bee. "I will be careful to always pay attention to where I am going and what I am doing."

Busy Bumble Bee's family
was very glad to see him.
They buzzed and buzzed
as they greeted him.

Mr. Loggerhead Turtle, Mr. Octopus,
Mr. Scallop, and Mr. Redfish
had been caring, reliable friends.

It is very special to be a caring,
reliable friend and help others in need.

18

ISLE OF ST. JAMES

Corn Landing

Moore Cottage

Wilson Beach

St. Teresa Beach

Stingray Point

oyster bars

Bay Mouth Bar

Peninsula Pt.

Alligator Harbor

N

W   E

S

GULF OF MEXICO

Alligator Point   Southwest Cape

The End.

Education Page

Loggerhead Turtle

The loggerhead is the most common sea turtle in Florida, but remains a "threatened species" because of habitat loss and drownings caused by shrimp trawls. An estimated 14,000 females nest in the Southeastern U.S. each year. The loggerhead is named for its large head. Adults weigh 200 to 300 pounds and measure about three feet in length. They use their powerful jaws to crush mollusks, crabs and encrusting animals.

Atlantic Coquina

Found in a whole rainbow of colors, just below the sand's surface at the surf line.

Scallop

Scallops are a marine bivalve (two shells joined together by a muscle) and are found in most of the world's oceans. They are highly prized for their food value. Most scallops are active swimmers and are the only migratory bivalve. The scallop swims by rapidly opening and closing its shell. Sometimes you can hear a soft popping sound as they open and close their shells.

Redfish (Red Drum)

Redfish are inshore species until they are about 4 years old, when
they join the nearshore population. The redfish is copper bronze in color with one
to many spots on its tail. Average size is approximately 27 inches and about 8 pounds.
They feed on crustaceans, fish and mollusks and live to be 20 years or more.

Lettered Olive

Found in the sand at the surf line.

Florida Fighting Conch

Often found feeding in colonies, typically
in sandy areas near grass beds.

Common Octopus

The common octopus has a unique appearance with its
massive bulbous head, large eyes and eight distinctive arms.
They range from 12 to 36 inches and may weigh up to 22
pounds. Fast swimmers, they release a cloud of black ink
as a defense mechanism. If they lose an arm it will regrow.
Considered the most intelligent invertebrate, it feeds on
crabs, crayfish and mollusks.

Bumble Bee

Bumble bees are social, flying insects with black and yellow body hairs, often in bands. The soft hair, called pile, covers their entire body, making them appear and feel fuzzy. Bumble bees feed on nectar and gather pollen to feed to their young. They are non-aggressive and will sting only in defense of their nest if harmed. The buzzing of the bumble bee is not caused by the beating of its wings, but rather the vibration of its flight muscles.

Finger Sponge

Also known as Dead Man's Fingers, it is best left on the beach.

Firefly (Lightning Bug)

Fireflies are members of the beetle family, usually brown and soft-bodied. Many fireflies use bioluminescence to attract mates or prey. The light they produce can be 96% efficient compared with an incandescent electric bulb, which is 10% efficient. (The other 90% of the energy produces heat.) While fireflies are found in many temperate and tropical environments around the world, the firefly-richest region in North America is the 30-mile swath on the Florida-Georgia border in the Big Bend Coast to the Okefenokee Swamp. In some areas, large groups of fireflies synchronize their flashes. In ancient Mayan culture, fireflies were associated with stars.

St. Teresa, Florida

St. Teresa is a beachfront community in Franklin County, Florida, located on the Gulf of Mexico and accessed by U.S. Highway 98. It is bordered on the east by Alligator Harbor and on the southeast by Alligator Point. Established in the 1870s as a summer retreat for residents of North Florida and South Georgia, St. Teresa has no commercial establishments, cannot be seen from the highway, and consists of approximately 100 (when established in the 1870s about 25) beachfront cottages, many of which have been in the same families for generations. Described as "heaven for dogs and children," it is a unique part of "Old Florida."

Alligator Point, Florida

Southwest Cape, known locally as Alligator Point, is located on Alligator Spit, a peninsula extending about 4.8 miles westward from Lighthouse Point at the southeast corner of St. James Island in Franklin County, Florida. Alligator Point is at the eastern end of Apalachee Bay, bordered on the north by Alligator Head and on the south by the Gulf of Mexico. It is bordered by several prominent offshore shoal systems, including Dog Island to the southwest and Ochlockonee Shoal to the east.

Carol, presenting **Marvin the Magnificent Nubian Goat** *to the Florida Governors Mansion Library. It is read to the visiting children.*

Carol was born in Live Oak, a small north Florida town halfway between Tallahassee and Jacksonville. Her ancestors arrived in the Live Oak area by covered wagon in the 1850s. Much of Carol's early life was spent in a rural environment, during which she developed her love of animals, especially farm animals.

She received her B.S. Degree in Elementary Education from Florida State University and taught second grade in Gainesville, Florida, while her husband Ed obtained his law degree.

Ed and Carol raised their three children on Moore Farm just outside of Tallahassee. While Moore Farm contained many animals including cows, horses, chickens, peacocks, turkeys, cats, dogs, and ducks, the family favorite was Marvin the pet goat. Marvin lived to be twelve years old and was an integral part of the Moore Farm.

Ed and Carol's seven grandchildren love to visit Nana and Dadaddy at their home in Tallahassee and their coast home at St. Teresa on the Gulf of Mexico.

Illustrator, Michael Harrell

Michael Harrell is a native of Tallahassee, Florida. He received a B.F.A. from the University of Georgia in 1989.

Harrell's seascapes and landscapes paintings can be found in private and corporate collections throughout the U.S. and abroad.

His oils and watercolors have been featured in many national publications, including *American Artist Watercolor* magazine, *American Art Collector*, and *The Artist's Magazine*. More than a dozen top galleries represent Harrell's work and, in 2004, *The Artist's Magazine* listed Michael Harrell as one of the top 20 artists in the United States to watch.

Michael Harrell's clients have included American Express, Paramount Pictures, Seaside, and the Mystic Seaport Museum.